TO: M_____

♡: EB

R.L. STINE'S HAUNTED LIGHTHOUSE

by R.L. Stine

A Parachute Press Book

Parachute Publishing, L.L.C. Busch Entertainment Corporation
156 Fifth Avenue 231 S. Bemiston Avenue
New York, NY 10010 Suite 600
Clayton, MO 63105-1914

A Parachute Press Book

A Special Barnes & Noble Edition

This book was created and produced by Parachute Publishing, L.L.C.
in cooperation with Busch Entertainment Corporation.

ISBN 0-7607-4807-1

First Printing: June 2003

Printed in Canada

www.buschgardens.com

www.seaworld.com

10 9 8 7 6 5 4 3 2 1

PART ONE

BOSTON
1879

CHAPTER 1

"I want to go home!" my sister, Annie, whined. She tugged at her dark curls. Annie is eight, but sometimes I think she acts like a two-year-old.

"We all want to go home, dear," Mother said. "Can't you try to be patient like your brother, William?"

William—that's me. I'm twelve. "Yes. Why can't you be perfect, like me?" I said, grinning in Annie's face.

Annie gave me a hard shove that sent me staggering back along the dock. She's a lot stronger than she looks!

Father scratched his stubbly beard and stared out at the dark ocean waters. "There's a storm brewing," he said. "The harbor is nearly empty. I don't know if we can find a ship to take us."

Father's name is Augustus Van Legge. But everyone calls him Gus. He is the best boat-builder on Cape Cod. Father sold a big fishing boat last week. So, to celebrate, he brought Mom and Annie and me down to Boston for a family vacation.

Boston was so busy and dirty and noisy. We could barely make our way through the crowded streets. And we were nearly run over by a runaway horse carriage!

Annie and I couldn't wait to return to our quiet home on the beach in Cape Cod. We missed our dog, Horatio. Also, it was Annie's birthday—and her present was waiting for her at home.

Mother shivered and held her wide-brimmed hat on her head with one hand.

"Get us home, Gus," she said. "The wind is blowing up something fierce, and there's a fog rolling in. There has got to be a ship of some kind."

"I'll look for the harbormaster," Father replied.

We found the harbormaster in a tiny whitewashed hut on the other side of the dock. He was a short, chubby man with shiny black hair and a patch over one eye. He sat on a tall stool behind a cluttered counter and frowned at Father.

"I must return home today," Father said. "My biggest customer is arriving first thing tomorrow morning."

"And it's my birthday!" Annie cried.

"I am sorry, good folks," the harbormaster said in a deep voice. "There is no one to take you today. The last ship set sail about an hour ago."

"But surely there must be someone to take us up the coast," Father replied.

The man motioned to the window. "Take a look at the harbor, mate. It is empty. I can't produce a ship out of thin air."

I felt sorry for Annie. I was cold and tired, too. And I kept thinking about Horatio. I knew he missed us.

We walked back out onto the dock. No one said a word. The wind grew colder. It made our clothes flap hard against our bodies. Mother held on to her hat tightly. A heavy fog had lowered around us. I could see that Annie was about to cry.

Squinting into the fog, I saw a dark shape bobbing on the water at the end of the dock. Slowly, the shape began to take form. The fog swirled around it. I gasped when I realized I was staring at a ship.

I rubbed my eyes. I thought I was dreaming. Where had it come from? Had it been hiding in the fog all along?

"Father—look." I tugged his coat sleeve.

Father let out a shout. "Can it be? A ship?"

He started to run, and we hurried after him, our shoes thudding on the wooden planks.

It was a four-masted schooner. As we came closer, I saw the name printed on the side— *Marie Dubois*.

"It's so big. Why didn't we see it before?" I asked. I didn't spy anyone on board. The sails whipped violently in the sudden bursts of wind.

Father stopped at the edge of the dock and called out. "Ahoy, there. Anyone aboard?"

A tall, bald-headed sailor wearing a white captain's uniform appeared on the deck. He stared down at us. The pipe in his mouth waved up and down.

"We are looking for passage to Cape Cod," Father shouted over the wind.

The sailor shook his head. "Not on this ship," he called.

"We will pay you well," Father replied.

"It's my birthday!" Annie shouted. "I want to go home!"

"Believe an old sea captain's word, ye don't want to travel on this ship," the man said.

"And why not?" Father asked.

The sailor narrowed his tiny, dark eyes at Father. "This ship is haunted," he said.

CHAPTER 2

"My name is Augustus Van Legge. I've built many a ship, and I've sailed with many a crew," Father said. "I've heard enough tales of haunted ships to know they are never true."

"My name be Ernest Malloy," the captain replied. "And I'm a son of a son of a sea dog. My word is all I have in this world, sir. And I am telling you this ship is haunted."

"Ernest Malloy," Father repeated the man's name. "Your name sounds familiar, but I don't think we've met. Well, carry us home, and we will test your word," Father said, reaching for his money purse. "If any ghost dare show his face in *this* wind, he will be blown away."

Was the ship really haunted? I held on to Annie. We were both trembling from the cold. But now I was trembling harder from the captain's words.

Sometimes late at night, as the fire crackled in the hearth, Father told us frightening stories about haunted ships and pirate ghosts who could never rest.

The stories sent cold shivers down my back. I didn't know if they were true or not. But I knew I never wanted to find out—even if Father was there to protect me.

"Aye, aye, come along, then," Malloy said finally. "Climb aboard and never say you weren't warned by an honest sea captain."

Annie and I glanced at each other. Were we really about to board a haunted ship?

Father helped Mother up to the swaying deck. Annie went next. My heart pounded as

I climbed the gangway and stepped onto the deck.

"Hoist the anchor! Hoist it now, mates!" Malloy shouted.

From out of nowhere, a crew of sailors scrambled onto the deck. They were ragged and dirty and unshaven men. Rough-looking. Mumbling to themselves, they set to work.

"We will pay well," Father told Malloy again.

"Yes, you will," the sailor replied in a whisper.

"What did he mean by that?" Annie asked.

We would soon find out.

I watched the sails slapping in the wind. The ship tossed and rocked as high waves splashed over the deck. Black storm clouds rolled overhead.

Father led Mother, Annie, and me to the cabin below deck. "You will be safe here as we ride out the storm," he said.

But as soon as he left, Annie and I ran

back up. We hid behind a black metal trunk. We didn't want to miss anything.

"Are those sailors all ghosts?" Annie whispered.

"Of course not," I said, but why was I trembling?

We watched Father take his place next to Captain Malloy at the wheel. "Rough weather!" Malloy shouted over the rush of the driving wind. "You'll need your sea legs today, mate."

Annie and I moved behind the main mast, struggling to keep our balance. "Are you afraid?" Annie asked me. "I am, a little."

"Why don't you go below with Mother?" I replied. I didn't want her to see how scared I was.

"No. I want to watch," she whispered.

We both cried out as the ship tilted nearly on its side. We threw our arms around the mast. Water frothed over the swaying deck. Slowly, the ship found its bearings.

I spotted a rope hammock near the stern.

I lifted Annie into it, then pulled myself up beside her. It felt safer to be swaying and tossing inside the hammock.

Lightning crackled overhead. Then a boom of thunder echoed over the ocean. The schooner rose up like a bucking stallion, then slapped back into the water.

My stomach lurched. I gripped the hammock ropes tightly with both hands and shut my eyes. I opened my eyes when the sailors began to sing. Their voices were deep and mournful, and the words they sang gave me a chill. . . .

"Every man is alone when he sails the sea.
In the storm-tossed waves, there is only me.

At night I pray before I sleep,
Don't let me go down in the briny deep.

The bottomless ocean calls a man to his doom—
One more, one more, there is always room.

*One more, one more, calls the cold, dark sea
And only the fish to say good-bye to me."*

I turned and saw that Annie was shivering, too. She huddled close to me and whispered, "I don't like that song. Why are they singing it? And why do the sailors all look so sad?"

I started to answer but stopped when I saw a sailor a mile above us in the topsail. He raised his arms in the air. Then, like a bird taking off, he leaped off the sail.

Annie and I both screamed as the man came plunging headfirst to the deck.

To our shock, he spun in midair and landed on his feet. He grinned at Annie and me and took a bow. I gasped as he strode up to the hammock. "Why don't *you* try it, lad?" he rasped.

"No! How did you do that?" I cried.

"How about a jump, boy?" he asked, a crooked grin on his face. He reached through the hammock and pinched my cheek. "How about showing us all what a lad can do?"

"No. Please . . ." I whispered.

He tossed his head back and laughed. Then he strode away, still grinning.

"I think I want to go below deck with Mother," Annie whispered.

"Me, too," I confessed, rubbing my sore cheek.

But before we could leave the hammock, a tall, lanky sailor with a short black beard and a toothless grin stepped up to us. "Good day, mates," he growled. "Where are ye heading?"

"To Cape Cod," I choked out.

"But where are ye heading?" he repeated. "I say, heading? Where are ye heading?"

As Annie and I stared at him, he removed his head and held it out to me. "Where are ye heading?" the head asked.

Annie and I opened our mouths in screams of horror.

The head laughed. The sailor turned and strode away, holding his head in front of him.

"Father! Father!" I screamed. I tried to scramble out of the hammock, but my legs were tangled in the ropes.

I looked up and saw the sailors moving fast. They surrounded Annie and me. They grabbed the hammock and began to twirl it, wrapping us inside it.

"Father! Help! Father!" I screamed.

But my voice was drowned out by the deep voices of the sailors. They began to sing again, swinging the rope hammock harder and harder. . . .

"The bottomless ocean calls a man to his doom—
One more, one more, there is always room."

Father came rushing to us across the tilt-ing deck. "Malloy—take control of your crew!" he shouted. "Malloy—?"

Father stopped suddenly and his mouth dropped open. "Now I remember where I heard your name before!" He turned to the captain. "Oh, for heaven's sake. For heaven's sake. Ernest Malloy. You and your men went down with your ship—a year ago in a storm off the coast of Maine. The ship sank and all men aboard were lost."

A cold smile spread over Malloy's stubbled face. "I told you the ship was haunted!"

CHAPTER 3

Trembling, Annie and I peered out from the knotted hammock. Father stuck his chest out and stood up to the grinning sea captain. "And what do you plan to do with us?" Father boomed.

"A dead man makes no plans," Malloy replied.

"You intend to cause us trouble?" Father demanded.

"You have caused your own trouble," said Malloy. "You are the cursed passengers of a dead man's ship."

Thunder roared. Lightning flashed so brightly, I blinked.

And when I opened my eyes, Malloy had vanished. I squinted out through the hammock ropes—and saw that all the sailors had vanished with him.

Thunder shook the deck. The ship rocked hard.

"They are still here," Father said. I could see the fear in his face. "We are not rid of them so easily."

I heard the invisible sailors laughing. Cold, cruel laughter.

"And now my sailing skills will truly be tested," Father said with a sigh. "I must guide us home through this storm. But can a living man sail a ghost ship?"

He untwistsed Annie and me and pulled us from the hammock.

Mother climbed up from the cabin below. "The storm is tossing the ship like a feather in the wind. Will we be safe, Gus?"

Father nodded. "I shall steer us *between* the raindrops!"

He made a proud boast, but his brow creased with worry.

For safety, Mother, Annie, and I tied our-selves to the masts. I told Mother about the ghostly sailors and how they had suddenly disappeared.

"We are well rid of them," she said. But her chin trembled and tears welled in her eyes.

Father stood behind the wheel, leaning forward into the wind and rain. He tested the wheel. "Yes! I can steer it!" he cried. He began to whip the wheel around frantically, strug-gling to keep us on course.

Father was a master seaman. I knew he could guide even a ghost ship home safely. But as I gripped the mast and watched him work the wheel, I could hear the ghostly sailors begin to sing again.

"One more, one more, calls the cold, dark sea
And only the fish to say good-bye to me."

Were the sailors planning to appear? Were they planning to harm us?

The ocean heaved us from side to side, drenching us with waves of icy water. Sometimes I could see eyes staring at us in the fog, eyes without faces. Once I saw the tall sailor's bearded, grinning head floating just above me.

"How about a jump, boy?" a gruff voice whispered in my ear. *"How about a leap? Let's see what a lad can do."*

"Please—leave me alone!" I shouted. "Leave me alone!"

How happy I was when Father finally exclaimed, "We are near! I can see the beacon from the lighthouse. It will guide us to the cove."

Mother, Annie, and I let out a cheer. We untied ourselves from the mast.

Squinting into the storm, I could see the light, a pale circle broken up by curtains of rain and mist. "Hang on, Annie," I said. "We are almost there. We are very close to home."

Father turned the wheel toward shore. Rocking on high waves, the ship bounced into the cove. I could see a weary smile on Father's face. His eyes were locked on the beam from the lighthouse.

And then the ship jolted hard.

I heard a crash, louder than the wind and waves. Then a deafening crunch of wood against stone.

The ship tilted up and crashed down with a thunderous roar.

I heard laughter. Harsh laughter from the unseen sailors.

"Oh—!" I was thrown into the mast. My head hit with a *thud*. I couldn't see. Dizziness swept over me. I dropped to my knees, struggling to shake it off.

Behind me, I could hear Annie crying. Mother's shouts to Father were drowned out by a roar of thunder.

I opened my eyes to see Father at my side.

"William, are you all right?" he asked, holding my shoulders. "I forgot about the rock shoals at the opening to the cove. We've hit the rocks. The boat is damaged. We . . . we're going down."

CHAPTER 4

The ship lurched hard, sending Father tumbling backward onto the deck. Lightning made the sky brighter than day.

"Are we going to drown?" Annie cried. "Are we going to die like those awful ghost sailors?"

Father didn't answer, at first. He scanned the ship and gasped. "No," he said, jumping to his feet. "There's a dinghy." He pointed to the tiny boat bobbing on the waves, tied to the side of the schooner. "It can take us to the island where the lighthouse stands."

I shielded my eyes from the rain and stared

at the lighthouse in the distance. It seemed so far away. Could that tiny boat carry us there safely?

Ernest Malloy spoke the truth, I thought. We brought ourselves only trouble by riding a dead man's ship. And now we were going to drown just like he and his sailors did.

Father must have read my thoughts. "Don't you give up hope, William," he said. "The dinghy is very small but it is sturdy. We will survive."

He lowered himself over the side of the schooner and dropped into the dinghy. It was a tiny wooden boat smaller than a canoe. He reached for Annie and pulled her down beside him. My poor little sister was soaked through and through.

Father reached for me, but I pulled away from him. "There's room for only three!" I cried. "What about Mother? There's room for only three!"

"Peg!" he called to Mother. "Peg, listen to

me. You can squeeze in. There's room in the bow."

Mother leaned over the rail. Her hat had blown away. Her golden hair was drenched, matted against her head. "No," she called down to him. "That little boat will sink if I try to squeeze in. I'll wait here, Gus. The ship has steadied itself. I know you will come back for me."

"I will take the children to shore then return," Father told her. "Do not worry, my darling. There will be plenty of time to get you to safety."

I saw Mother's hands grip the rail so tightly, her knuckles bulged. She bit her bottom lip. "Take them now," she called. "Take them quickly, Gus."

We made the treacherous trip over the waves in the dinghy. Father rowed as hard as he could, leaning into the wind.

Annie and I gripped the sides of the boat with all our might.

I watched Mother back in the schooner, kept my eyes on her until she vanished into the darkness. The little dinghy rocked and dipped and bounced us up and down, but it stayed afloat.

Drenched and breathless, we finally made it to the rocky shore of the island. My heart pounded so hard, I could hear it over the crashing waves.

I crawled out of the dinghy and onto the rocks. Then I turned and pulled Annie out of the boat and onto shore.

Above us, the lighthouse stretched up to the sky. Its light cut through the torrential rain, sending bright stripes through the black sky.

"Wait in the lighthouse. Wait for me there," Father said. "I shall return with your mother."

The last words I ever heard him say.

CHAPTER 5

I grabbed Annie's hand, and we started to pull ourselves over the slippery rocks to the little house beside the lighthouse tower. Rain battered us and drove us back. I was shivering so hard, I could barely walk.

I heard Annie's teeth chattering. In a flash of bright lightning, I saw the terror on her face.

At the door to the lighthouse, we both turned back to the ocean. Shielding my eyes with my hand, I could see Father in the dinghy, tossed from side to side like a kite in a windy sky. The schooner was a black shadow far on the horizon.

The wind howled around the side of the lighthouse. It made a mournful sound like the cry of a dog. I brushed rainwater from my eyes.

And when I looked back to the sea, Father was gone.

"Where is he? Where is Father?" Annie screamed, squeezing my hand.

"He is doing well," I said, ignoring my thudding heartbeats. "He has nearly reached the schooner."

And then we saw the schooner begin to move. Away. Away from the island—as if torn away from us.

Carried by an invisible force, a powerful riptide.

Father gone.

The schooner carried away.

Annie and I stood shivering on the rocks, staring into the storm.

I heard a loud crash, but I didn't see the wave.

An explosion of sound, as if the world were cracking apart.

And then the wave swept over the rocky shore. And a wall of seawater roared over Annie and me.

It lifted us . . . carried us . . . swarmed over us completely.

And we were lost inside it . . . lost . . .

When I opened my eyes, I was sprawled in front of the lighthouse door. I raised my head, blinking away water, and saw Annie flat on the slick rocks beside me.

"Annie—?" My voice came out in a choked whisper. I pulled myself to my knees. I shook my head hard, trying to clear it.

Thunder rumbled, in the distance now. The rain had lightened to a cold drizzle. "Father told us to wait inside," I said. "We should go there."

I pulled my sister to her feet. She kept shaking her head, dazed. I raised my fist and pounded on the wooden door. "Is anyone in there?" I shouted. "Please let us in."

I turned back to search for my parents. But I could see no sign of the dinghy or the schooner in the high waves. I hoped that they were okay. I had to hold hope. . . .

Annie and I pounded on the door—and it slid open a crack. With a startled groan, I leaned into it and pushed it far enough for us to squeeze inside.

"Anyone here?"

"Hello?"

No answer.

Lightning flashed along a row of windows. In the sudden light, I spotted a lantern on a short square table. I crossed the room and picked it up. I found a big bag of wooden matches beside it. Fumbling to strike a match with my wet hands, I lit the lantern and held it above my head.

In the orange light, I could see a comfortable looking room. Paintings of ocean scenes on the wall. A leather couch and chairs. A stuffed swordfish mounted over a doorway. A suit of armor . . .

At the far wall, a wooden stairway curved up from the room, leading to the light tower. A pile of burlap sandbags was stacked at the bottom of the stairs.

"People must live here," Annie said. "But where are they?"

We shouted again, louder this time. But again, no answer.

"Maybe they left the island when they saw the storm coming," I told Annie. My legs were trembling. A shudder ran down my body. I hoped my sister could not see how scared I was.

Annie gazed up the curving stairs. "Maybe they are up there."

"Helloooo?" My voice echoed up the tower. Grabbing the metal rail, I started to climb, holding the lantern in my free hand. I followed the stairs as they curved steeply up the tower.

"Please, William—wait for me," Annie called.

I slowed my pace. I listened to my sister's shoes thudding on the wooden stair rungs.

"I am so worried about Mother and Father," she said, her voice echoing against the stone walls. "They should have been here by now."

"Father said to wait in here," I replied. "And so we shall."

"But I think I saw the ship being carried away," Annie said.

I felt a tremble of fear, but I kept my voice steady for my sister's sake. "Father is an expert sailor. He will bring the dinghy back to the island. He and Mother will meet us here. We have to be patient and wait."

We continued to climb in silence. The only sounds were the wind howling outside around the tower and the heavy thud of our shoes on the stairs.

Finally, we reached the top. I raised the

lantern. We were standing in a bare round room. I saw a stiff-backed wooden chair. A low table beside it.

"No one up here," Annie whispered. "No one in the lighthouse—except for us. How strange."

"Mother and Father will be here soon," I said. "The lighthouse will give us shelter. We can wait here until the storm has ended."

Annie frowned. "But what if they—?" she started to say.

"Shhh." I raised a finger to my lips. In the lantern light, I saw something on the table. A sheet of paper.

A letter? A note?

The floorboards creaked under my shoes as I walked to the table. I picked up the thick sheet of paper, held it to the lantern, and squinted at the words printed by hand on the page.

"Oh—!" I uttered a gasp. The paper fluttered from my hand and went sailing down the tower stairs. But the words on the page would remain with me forever. . . .

The bottomless ocean calls a man to his doom—
One more, one more, there is always room.

PART TWO

CAPE COD TODAY

CHAPTER 6

"Oh, wow. I burned mine!" My brother, Mike, pulled the stick from the fire. His marshmallow flamed up for a second, then the fire faded. "Yuck. Black gunk on a stick," he complained.

"Well, try another one," I said. I tossed him a fresh marshmallow. "You interrupted Cap'n Jack's ghost story."

Cap'n Jack raised his admiral's cap and scratched his woolly hair. His bearded face flickered in the dancing flames. "It's getting late," he said. "The story will keep. My stories keep better than the fish I sell."

"But what happened to the two kids?" I asked. "Did their parents return to rescue them from the lighthouse?"

Cap'n Jack shook his head. "No, they didn't, Ashley. The riptide took that schooner, tore it from the rock, and swallowed it whole. With Van Legge and his wife aboard."

"The parents died?" Mike bit his lip as he stared at the marshmallow roasting in the fire.

Cap'n Jack nodded. "The kids were dead, too. Only they didn't know it."

"Huh?" Was I shivering from the cold of the night, or from Cap'n Jack's ghost story?

"The high wave that washed over them took their lives. They didn't even realize it." He poked his pipe at my shoulder. "And one other thing they didn't realize."

"What's that?" I asked.

"The light in the lighthouse tower had gone out. The island lay in darkness. Even if they had survived, there was no way the parents could have found the island."

Cap'n Jack climbed to his feet and stretched. He was tall and lanky, and his sailor pants were too short for him. When he stretched, all his bones cracked. He pointed out to the ocean. Mike and I turned and squinted to where he was pointing.

I could see the outline of the dark light-house. It stood on the tiny rock island just off shore.

"That was over a hundred years ago," Cap'n Jack said. "No one has lived there since. No one can stand the wails of those sad ghost children, still waiting for their parents to return."

Mike and I helped Cap'n Jack put out the campfire. I turned to Cap'n Jack. "Can we come back tomorrow night?"

"Do you know any more scary stories?" Mike asked.

Cap'n Jack grinned. "Does a fish have lips?"

The next afternoon, I spread out a beach blanket, cranked up the boom box, and sprawled on my back, eager to catch some rays. I'm thirteen and Mike is ten. Our family has been coming to the Cape since I was six.

Today was the first really sunny day. We had been here nearly a week, and I was still as pale as those marshmallows we roasted last night.

My crazy brother was busy chasing seagulls off the beach. I explained to him that it was their beach, too. But Mike said he was bored, and if he wanted to chase seagulls it was none of my business.

Behind us on the dune, I could see Cap'n Jack fiddling around in his beach shack. He was polishing the hand-lettered sign that read CAP'N JACK'S BAIT SHOP & BOAT RENTAL.

I heard a squawk and saw seagulls scatter in front of my brother. He came running up to me, kicking sand on my blanket. "What's your problem?" I asked.

"You are," he said. I raised my head from the blanket. I could see Mike staring out at the lighthouse. "Ashley, you know that story Cap'n Jack was telling last night? It couldn't be true, could it? I mean, about the light-house being haunted?"

I groaned. "Now you believe in ghosts, Mike? How do you feel about the tooth fairy?"

"But he said people hear cries from the lighthouse. Kids crying. Maybe—"

"I think you should swim out there and see for yourself," I said. "Maybe *you* could haunt the place for a while."

"Ha-ha, Ashley. You are *so* not funny." He tossed something onto my stomach.

Yuck! A disgusting horseshoe crab!

"Get out of here!" I heaved it at him.

Laughing like a hyena, he went running to the shore.

I settled down on the blanket and pulled my sunglasses over my eyes. The sun felt so warm and friendly. I gazed up at the slow-moving puffs of cloud.

A short while later, I had the strange feeling that someone was watching me. I sat up—and stared at a thin, dark-haired boy I'd never seen before.

And this is where my story turns scary. . . .

CHAPTER 7

"Hi," I said. "Where'd *you* come from?"

"I live around here," he said.

I pulled myself up and straightened the top of my bikini. "Oh. We're just vacationers," I said. "Summer people. I'm Ashley. That kid chasing seagulls is my brother, Mike."

"I'm Edgar," he said. "Why is your brother chasing seagulls?"

"He's crazy."

Edgar smiled. He had a nice smile. He brushed back his straight black hair. He wasn't dressed for the beach. He had on a blue, long-sleeved shirt over black pants.

"Are you enjoying the sun?" he asked.

I nodded. "You bet."

"Hey, Ashley!" Cap'n Jack shouted from the top of the dune. "I'm outta here for a while. The bluefish are runnin'—and I want to try to catch up to them!"

"Good luck!" I called. I watched him hurry off, carrying a fishing rod in each hand.

"Hey, what's up?" Mike came trotting over, kicking sand on my blanket again.

"This is Edgar," I said. "He lives here."

"Sweet," Mike said. "Maybe we can hang out. The beach has been empty. None of our friends have arrived yet."

Edgar smiled again. "Yes. We can hang out."

"Maybe we can build a fire again tonight," Mike said. "And Cap'n Jack could tell us more stories about the ghosts that haunt the lighthouse."

"Stories that *some* ignorant people actually believe," I said, sneering at Mike.

Hi, I'm Mike. I love scary ghost stories.

But my sister, Ashley, doesn't.

This is
Cap'n Jack.
He owns a
beach shack,
and he likes
to tell us
scary stories.

Ashley and I went to the local lighthouse—something weird was definitely going on there.

We made two new friends who turned out to be *very* scary.

Then we met their
parents. This was
one creepy family!

A vacation we'll never forget!

To my surprise, Edgar stared hard at me. "You don't believe the story about the lighthouse? Everyone here knows it's true."

"Yeah, sure," I said, rolling my eyes. "Tell me another one."

"No, I'm serious," Edgar said. "People here have seen the ghost kids."

"Have *you* seen them?" Mike asked.

Edgar nodded. "Yes. They usually come out for a while at sundown." He turned to me. "Want to see them?"

"You're kidding, right?" I asked.

Edgar motioned to the canoes piled up next to Cap'n Jack's shack. "It's a short boat ride away. You can see for yourself."

"Let's do it!" Mike cried. "Come on, Ashley. There's nothing else to do."

He was right. So far, this vacation had been totally boring. "Okay, okay," I said. "But I think the whole thing is stupid."

"What if we see real ghosts?" Mike asked. "Wouldn't that be totally cool?" He tugged at my arm. "Come on, Ashley. Let's do it. Let's go."

I glanced up at the sky. Dark clouds had rolled over the sun. I sighed. "Okay. Let's go."

Biggest mistake of my life?

In a word, yes.

CHAPTER 8

I scribbled a note for Cap'n Jack. I told him
we borrowed a canoe to go to the lighthouse.

Mike and I dragged the canoe to the water.
Edgar climbed into the back with the paddles.

"We needed some excitement," Mike said.
"I can't wait to see the ghosts!"

"Cool your jets," I told him. "It's just a boring old lighthouse. Every lighthouse in the
world probably has a ghost story told about it."

"But this one is true," Edgar insisted. "Everyone knows it's true."

I turned in the canoe and stared at him.
He had a sly smile on his face.

Mike was so excited, he could barely sit still. "Do you really think we'll see William and Annie?" He grabbed the oars and started to paddle.

Edgar nodded and smiled at me again.

The lighthouse rose like a gray skyscraper ahead of us. The clouds grew darker. I felt a cold raindrop on my forehead. And then more rain began to patter down.

"We get these sudden storms all the time here on the Cape," Edgar said. "It'll blow over in no time."

But the rain pelted down harder, and the ocean began to swirl, tossing up big waves. Our little canoe bounced around like a soccer ball.

"Maybe we should head back," I shouted over the roar of the waves.

Edgar kept his eyes straight ahead. "We're nearly there."

The black rocks of the island sparkled like dark jewels. As we floated closer, I could see the square white house next to the light-house tower.

"I suppose you're going to tell us the ghost kids live in that little house," I said, rolling my eyes again.

Edgar didn't reply. I don't think he could hear me over the rain and wind.

Wisps of dark mist rose up from the island. Fingers of fog reached out, as if pulling us inside.

"Mike—are you okay?" I asked my brother.

He didn't answer. He had a frightening expression on his face. He pulled hard at the oars.

The heavy, damp fog swept around us.

The canoe hit against the rock shore. "We're here!" Edgar cried. He jumped out of the canoe and splashed his way onto the rocks.

Ducking against the rain, I followed him to shore. We both grabbed the bow of the canoe and struggled to drag it onto the rocky island.

"Hey, wait—!" I shouted at Mike. "You know, this would be a lot easier for Edgar and me if you'd get out of the boat!"

He didn't move.

"Mike?" I said.

He didn't move. He didn't look up.

"Mike—!" I shouted. "Are you okay?"

CHAPTER 9

"Mike—what's wrong? Tell me what's wrong!"

Slowly, he raised his head. "Can't move. I . . . I think I'm seasick." He leaned his head over the side of the boat.

"Give me a break," I said. "You can't be sea-sick. We're on *land*."

He groaned. "Maybe I'm landsick!"

I gave the canoe a hard tug. "Come on. Get out of there. This was your idea, remember? Hurry. It's really storming."

Holding his stomach, Mike lowered him-self from the canoe.

I turned and saw Edgar running to the little house behind the lighthouse tower. "Hey, wait up!" I shouted.

The rain really started to pound down just as we reached the front door. "Is it open?" I asked.

Edgar nodded. "Nobody has lived here for a hundred years—remember?" He pushed the door open all the way. "Except for the ghosts."

"Ha-ha," I murmured.

We stepped into the front room. Edgar latched the door behind us. Windows lined the wall that looked out to the ocean. The glass was missing or broken. Wooden shutters banged noisily, blown by the storm winds.

Mike found a light switch on the front wall. He clicked it up and down several times. "No lights," he whispered.

"There's no power," Edgar said. "Oh, look. A lantern." He pointed to a low table.

I found a bag of wooden matches on the

table. I lighted a match against the side of the table, then lowered the flame to the lantern wick. The oil inside caught fire, and the lantern glowed with an orangy light.

I started to raise the lantern, but Mike grabbed it out of my hand. "Hey—"

"I want to hold it!" Raising the light in front of him, he started running around the room. "Check out this place! Is this cool or what?"

Large paintings of ships and ocean scenes covered the walls. Two armchairs and a worn couch faced the fireplace. A three-foot-long swordfish was mounted high above the mantel.

Mike stopped in front of a suit of armor and raised the lantern to see it better. "Whoa. Do you believe this? Just like in Cap'n Jack's story."

"Why is a suit of armor in a lighthouse?" I asked.

"It probably belonged to the people who built the place," Edgar said.

Mike stared at the silvery visor pulled down over the helmet. "Think there's a ghost in there?"

My gaze rested on the long sword gripped in the iron-mesh glove. The metal arm was raised. The sword was poised, ready to attack.

I checked out a stack of old sailing books. "It's so weird," I murmured. "The lighthouse has been abandoned for over a hundred years, right? But this room looks as if someone was living here yesterday."

"The ghosts," Edgar whispered.

"Yeah, sure," I said. I don't believe in ghosts, but I was starting to get creeped out.

I moved to the mantel. I picked up a china vase shaped like a mermaid, its color faded. I started to set it down—when my eyes caught the shadow on the wall.

An enormous hand. A ghostly hand! Moving quickly, reaching out to grab me!

CHAPTER 10

I let out a squeal. Spun around.

And saw Mike crouched on the floor, wiggling his hand in front of the old lantern. He giggled, pleased with himself.

"Very funny," I said. "Bet you can do a bunny rabbit too. You're so clever, Mike."

But the old lighthouse was starting to really scare me. A clap of thunder made me jump.

I moved along the wall, closing the shutters. The little house creaked and groaned as the storm battered it. "It is so cold and damp in here," I said. "I wish I'd worn something heavier than this T-shirt." I rubbed my bare arms.

"Shhhh. You have to be very quiet to hear the ghosts," Edgar said.

I rolled my eyes. "How do *you* know so much about them?" I asked.

"I wrote a report about them last year for school," Edgar replied.

"Well, how do we know if we hear them?" Mike asked. "What do they sound like?"

"They sound like this," Edgar said. He cupped his hands around his mouth and went, "Owoooooooooo!"

I laughed. "Like ghosts in a Saturday morning cartoon?"

Edgar ignored me. He kept his hands cupped around his mouth and gave another ghostly howl. "Owooooo!"

Mike joined in. The two of them tilted back their heads and howled.

I shook my head. "This is totally dumb."

But I gasped when I heard another voice. A higher-pitched voice. A girl's voice!

"Owooooooo!"

Where was it coming from? The soft wail seemed to echo all around the room!

Mike and Edgar heard it, too. They stopped howling. Mike's eyes bulged and his mouth hung open.

"Owoooooooooo!"

The howl was so soft, so sad. A whisper, close and distant at the same time.

It sent a shiver down my back. My heart started to race.

A shutter banged open. A burst of wind and rain roared into the room. The lantern flickered.

Mike rushed to latch the shutter.

"Owooooooooooo."

Another chill rolled down my back. My arms were cold, covered with goose bumps.

Wind whipped through the room. Another shutter banged open. Then another. Mike and I struggled to pull them shut.

Behind us, we heard another eerie howl.

"Owoooooo."

Thunder boomed close overhead. The shutters banged again.

I turned to the sound of the howl. "Oh, wait," I said. "Wait a minute!"

I stepped up to the suit of armor.

"Ashley, what are you doing?" Mike asked in a trembling voice.

"That isn't a ghost howl," I said. "It's wind. It's wind blowing through the helmet on the suit of armor."

"Are y-you sure?" Mike stammered.

"Watch," I said. I raised my hands. Grabbed the visor on the front of the helmet. And lifted it up.

CHAPTER 11

The wailing stopped.

I turned back to the two boys. "Sorry, guys. No ghosts. Just the wind through the visor."

I breathed a sigh of relief. I don't believe in ghosts. But the howling had me freaked.

Mike gaped at me, his mouth still open. "Did it really stop?"

"Yes, it stopped. Don't be such a baby."

"*Owooooooo.*" Another soft wail, so high and pretty—behind me!

Startled, I let go of the visor. It dropped against the helmet with a loud *clang*.

The suit of armor trembled.

I heard a sudden creaking noise.

I saw Mike drop the lantern. He dove at me—and shoved me out of the way—

—as the sword came slicing down!

Mike and I tumbled over each other. With a heavy *thud,* the sword blade cut into the floorboard, inches away from us.

Still gripped in the iron glove of the armor, it remained in the floor. Inches away . . . inches from me . . .

"Whoa!" My heart thudded in my chest. I couldn't move. I stared in horror at the heavy sword. "Mike, you saved my life!"

He climbed to his feet. He brushed off his knees. "Yeah. I guess I did. Wow." With a sigh, he slumped hard against the mantel.

As Mike bumped the mantel, I saw the stuffed swordfish move, a few feet above his head.

It tipped forward, its saw-blade snout aimed down at Mike's head.

I let out a scream as it began to fall.

I jumped to my feet and barreled into Mike, sending him sprawling. The swordfish came crashing down. Its saw stuck into the floor, and the fish stayed there, standing on its head.

"You . . . you—" Mike stammered.

"—saved *your* life?" I finished the sentence for him.

We stared at each other, both breathing hard, both not believing what had just happened to us.

"Two close calls," Edgar said, starting to pace back and forth with his hands in his pants pockets. "This isn't good. Maybe we disturbed the ghosts."

"Edgar, those were accidents," I said. "I touched the suit of armor and made its arm fall. Then Mike bumped the mantel and the swordfish fell off the wall."

Edgar narrowed his eyes at me. "Accidents? Do you really think so?"

"*Owooooooooo.*" Once again, the eerie wail floated through the room.

I shuddered. "I don't care what it is," I said. "I think it's time to leave."

"But we just got here," Edgar protested. "We came all this way. Don't you want to see the ghosts? Don't you want to meet William and Annie?"

I turned to my brother. "Mike, are you ready to go back?"

He glanced at the swordfish stuck in the floor. "Yeah, I guess."

I strode to the door with the two boys close behind. The rusted latch was stuck, but I managed to shove it open. I pulled open the door and stepped outside.

The sky was inky, nearly as black as night, but the rain had stopped. Tall waves crashed on the rocky shore of the island.

Raising my eyes to the mainland, I could see lights dotting the shore. Mom and Dad were probably wondering why we didn't come home when it started to rain. I wished I were there in the cottage with them, cozy and warm. I couldn't wait to get off this dark, frightening island.

I started to run toward the water. "Mike, I'll row back," I said. But then I stopped.

And stared in shock. "Oh, no!" I cried. "Our canoe—it's gone!"

CHAPTER 12

Lightning flashed. I stared at the bare black rocks, glistening from the rain.

Mike slipped beside me and grabbed my hand. "How are we going to get home?" he whispered.

I shook my head. "We'll think of something."

"We'd better go back inside the lighthouse," Edgar said.

Thunder roared as we stepped back into the lighthouse. Edgar closed the door behind us and latched it again. I hugged myself, trying to warm up. "It's so cold in here. Maybe we could start a fire," I said.

Edgar frowned. "There's no wood. What could we burn?"

Before I could answer, I heard a voice. A girl singing a slow, sad song in a gentle voice . . .

"Alone I shall be, alone I shall stay.
Won't someone turn my lonely night into day. . . ?"

I gasped. The singing seemed to float down from the top of the tower. "Who's there?" I called. "Who's up there?"

I heard footsteps on the curving stairs. Soon, two black shoes appeared, then a long gray skirt dragging over the stairs, then a high-collared white blouse.

A sad-looking girl with curly, soft brown hair appeared. She stepped lightly over the pile of sandbags at the bottom of the stairs. She stared at Mike and me without smiling.

"Wh-who are you?" I stammered. "How did you get up there?"

"Don't be afraid," Edgar said. "That's my sister, Annabel."

Annabel nodded her head in greeting. She was about Mike's age, maybe a little younger. She had a pale, pretty face and mournful, dark eyes.

"You were up there all along?" I cried. "You were making those ghost sounds to scare Mike and me?"

"Oh, we were just having a little fun," Annabel replied.

"Fun? Scaring innocent people is fun?" Mike demanded angrily.

"You scared us both to death," I said.

Annabel frowned. "Welcome to the club," she whispered.

"Excuse me?" I said. "What do you mean?"

Annabel turned to her brother. "Oh, dear. They haven't caught on yet. I suppose we'd better just tell them."

"We're the ghosts," Edgar said.

I rolled my eyes. "Hel-lo? What kind of

idiots do we look like?" I turned to Mike. "Big joke. They're only trying to scare us."

"I know," Mike said. "The ghost kids were named William and Annie."

"Annie is short for Annabel," the girl said.

"And my name is William Edgar Van Legge," the boy said. "I called myself Edgar to trick you into coming to the island."

"I don't believe you," I said, crossing my arms in front of me. "Prove it."

"No problem," Edgar replied. He shut his eyes—and his head popped off his shoulders. It rose up to the ceiling, then dropped into his hands. He lifted it back onto his neck and grinned at me.

Annabel opened her mouth wide—wider, wider—and a huge purple tongue, fat as a snake, shot out at me. Then she pulled the tongue back into her mouth and popped out both of her eyes. They bobbed in front of Mike and me, then slid back into her head.

"Okay. I believe you. I believe in ghosts.

Okay? There. I said it. I believe in ghosts," I said, backing away on trembling legs.

"I believe you, too," Mike said, trying to hide behind me. "You're the ghosts. Please—no more proof!"

William and Annabel burst out laughing. Cold, cruel laughter that echoed off the tower walls.

They stood side by side, grinning at Mike and me. Slowly, they began to move toward us. Closer . . . closer . . .

"What do you want?" I cried. "Why did you bring us here? What are you going to do to us?"

CHAPTER 13

"We just want to be friends," Annabel said. She and her brother backed us to the wall.

"We're so lonely here," William said.

"Okay. No problem. We're friends," I said.

We have to get out of here! I thought. *We have to get away from them!*

"Are you going to let us go?" Mike asked.

"You don't understand," William said, staring at us coldly. "We need real friends. *Ghost* friends."

"It's not so bad once you get used to it," his sister added. "You can fly . . . walk right through walls . . . make wonderful faces. . . ." She scrunched up her face into a snarling monster.

I leaped back.

"It won't take long to become ghosts," William said. "It won't hurt that much. And then we can all be friends . . . friends forever."

A chill rolled down my back. I grabbed Mike's hand. "We're outta here!" I said.

Pulling my brother after me, I took off, running to the door. Frantically, I grabbed for the latch. It wouldn't budge.

I turned to see the two ghosts floating slowly, steadily toward us. "We can't let you go," Annabel said. "We need you to be our friends."

"NO—!" I screamed. I pulled Mike to the stairs. We started to run up the curving steps, taking them two at a time.

"You can't escape from us up there, Ashley," Annabel called. "If you go up the tower, there's only one way out—and that's *down*. All the way down."

"Do you want to jump?" William demanded. "If you do, we can all be friends."

Gasping for breath, I pulled myself up the steep, curving staircase.

"We're right behind yooou," William howled.

I glanced down and saw the ghosts coming after us, floating up the stairs. They had such cold, evil grins on their pale faces.

My legs felt rubbery and weak. But I forced myself to keep going.

"We can't escape them," Mike said, climbing hard. "What are we going to do?"

We reached the top. I gazed out the small round window. So far down to the ground. Too far . . .

"What's that?" I stared at the ocean—and saw a bright green glow far out at sea. Slowly, slowly, it rose up through the fog and took shape.

"A schooner!" I cried. "I see it! A four-masted schooner. Just like the one Cap'n Jack described!"

Annabel and William floated to the window. Their eyes were wide with shock. "It's them! It's Mother and Father!"

"Now your parents will find you," I said. "Aren't you happy? You will all be back together."

"No, we won't," Annabel whispered. She spun away from the window. I saw tears in her eyes. "No, we won't."

"They've been searching for us for over a hundred years," William said, his voice trembling. "But they can't find us. We're trapped here forever."

"Why do you say that?" I cried. "I can see their ship out there. I can see it so clearly."

"But they can't see us," Annabel explained. "There's no beacon to guide them."

"The lighthouse light has been out since we arrived. It's been out for over one hundred years," William said. "Without the light, they will never find us."

Annabel burst into tears. She pressed her

hands over her face and sobbed. William turned his face away. He didn't want us to see him cry.

I suddenly felt so sorry for both of them. What a horrible, lonely time they'd spent here.

"Well, just turn on the beacon!" Mike exclaimed. He pointed to a large metal switch sticking out of the tower wall. "That must be the switch. Just turn it on."

"We can't," William said. "We're ghosts, remember? We don't have the strength. The switch is stuck. Whenever we try to pull it down, it uses up all our energy, and we just disappear. Then it takes days for us to get our energy back."

Annabel gazed longingly out the window. "Mother and Father are so close. But it doesn't matter. They could be a million miles away."

"Well, *I'm* real," I said. "I can throw the switch."

Annabel gasped. "You'd help us? Really?

Even after we tried to terrify you to death?"

"Of course I'll help you," I said. "I feel so sorry for you both. I'll do whatever I can."

I grabbed the switch with both hands and tugged down on it.

And tugged.

And tugged.

Leaning into it, I tugged with all my strength.

"Oh, no," I moaned. "It's stuck. I can't move it."

CHAPTER 14

Annabel let out a sigh. "I knew it was too good to be true," she said. "Look—the ship is turning around. Mother and Father cannot see us."

"That means you'll have to stay here after all," William said. "You'll have to stay with us forever and be our friends."

I started to protest—but I heard a cracking sound.

Where is that coming from? I wondered.

Silence. Then another *crack,* longer this time. Louder.

Beneath me? Yes.

The stair beneath my feet splintered in two. I let out a shrill scream as I started to plunge down.

My hands shot out. I grabbed wildly for the switch. I wrapped both hands around it as I fell.

"WHOOOOOAAAA!"

I clung to the switch. My feet dangled in the air.

My hands started to slip. I knew I couldn't hold on for long.

It's so far down! I'll break my neck! Hold on, Ashley. Hold on!

Gripping the switch with all my might, I started to drop—and my weight pulled the switch down.

The two ghosts let out a happy cry as the lighthouse beacon flared on. "Ashley, you did it! You did it!" William cried. "The schooner—it's turning around! They see the light! They see us!"

"Finally!" Annabel exclaimed.

"Help me! I . . . can't hold on!" I shouted. "I'm going to fall!"

Annabel floated off the stairway. She moved beneath me and stretched out her arms. "Let go, Ashley. I'll catch you."

Too late.

My hands slipped off the switch, and I dropped straight down.

CHAPTER 15

Down . . . down . . . I plunged through the tower.

"Ahhhh!" I screamed all the way down.

I landed hard. My breath shot out of me.

Then everything went black. For how long? I don't know.

"Ashley! Ashley!" I suddenly heard Mike call out my name, but his voice seemed so far away.

I struggled to open my eyes. Struggled to breathe.

Finally, I sat up, blinking, gasping for air.

"Am I a ghost?" I choked out.

"Ashley, you're okay!" Mike shouted from

the top of the tower. "You landed on those sandbags."

Still dazed, I pulled myself to my feet.

Mike came running down the curved staircase. The two ghosts floated after him. "The schooner is close to shore," Annabel said. "Thank you, Ashley. Thank you for helping us." She hugged me. Her arms felt so light, so cold.

Mike pulled open the lighthouse door, and all four of us hurried outside. The rain had stopped, but lightning flickered high in the sky. The schooner appeared to float above the waves inside a glowing green cloud.

William and Annabel jumped up and down excitedly. "Mother! Father! We're here!" William shouted.

"Who's there?" a gruff voice called. "Mike? Ashley? Is that you?"

Startled, I turned to see Cap'n Jack pulling a rubber dinghy onto the rocks. He turned and squinted at us from beneath his beat-up admiral's hat. "So, there you are!"

"Cap'n Jack—you found us!" I cried. "We were trapped here and—"

Cap'n Jack hugged Mike and me. "You had me very worried," he said. "Very worried, going out in the storm like this, don't you know?"

"We're perfectly okay," I said. "We—"

"I wasn't worried about you," Cap'n Jack replied. "I didn't want to lose a good canoe!"

Mike and I laughed. We knew he was kidding. We were so happy to see him.

Cap'n Jack turned to the ghosts. "Who are you two? I don't recall seeing you around here. Summer tourists, are you?"

"No. They live here," I said.

Cap'n Jack's eyes narrowed in confusion. "Live here? On the lighthouse island? No one lives on this island."

We didn't have time to explain. A voice shouted from the ghost ship.

"Hallllooooo!"

We all turned to watch the ghostly schooner pull close to shore inside the eerie green glow of mist. As it bobbed on the waves, two figures waved from the ship.

We all stared as a man and woman, holding hands, floated over the water. The father wore a blue sea captain's uniform. His wife wore an old-fashioned suit, the skirt flowing down to her ankles, rippling in the wind as she floated so easily in the air.

"Mother! Father!" the ghost kids floated out to meet their parents.

Cap'n Jack, Mike, and I stared at them as they hugged each other in midair. All four of them were laughing and crying at the same time.

They formed a circle with their arms around one another. Flying above the water, they all spoke at once. They were so eager to tell their stories. So happy to be reunited.

"I'd be happy, too," Mike whispered, "if I hadn't seen Mom and Dad for a hundred years!"

"I'll bet Mom and Dad are worried about

us," I said. "How will we ever explain what happened?"

"We couldn't see the island till the beacon came on," I heard Mr. Van Legge say.

"We've been sailing all this time," Mrs. Van Legge added through her tears. "We never gave up hope."

"We waited here, just as you told us," Annabel said.

"We never gave up hope, either," William added.

"No storm will ever separate us again," Mr. Van Legge said.

I watched in amazement as the four ghosts floated down to the island. They were still talking, still holding hands.

But suddenly, the father broke away. He turned and stepped toward Cap'n Jack, Mike, and me. His expression was stern. He narrowed his eyes at us. "Now what will we do with you three?"

CHAPTER 16

I swallowed and stepped back.

What did he mean?

Slowly, a smile spread over his face and his blue eyes crinkled. "How can I ever thank you?" he said. "My children say that you turned on the lighthouse beacon for them."

"You brought our family back together," said Mrs. Van Legge. "Is there anything we can do to repay you?"

"No. Of course not," I said. "We were happy to help and—"

"Well, let me think," Cap'n Jack interrupted. He rubbed his scraggly beard. "You've been sailing back and forth over these waters a long time, isn't it the truth?"

Mr. Van Legge nodded. "Aye, we have."

Cap'n Jack squinted at him. "Perhaps you wouldn't mind telling me if you've seen any buried treasure anywhere about?"

Mr. Van Legge grinned at him. "As a matter of fact, I have seen something that might interest you, sir. There's a sunken ship just past Smuggler's Cove, between the two rocks. It's full of gold and jewels and pirate booty— or so they say."

Cap'n Jack let out a shout. "Yes! Yes!" He pumped his fists in the air. "Millions and millions of dollars in buried treasure! Do you know what I'll do with all that money? Good-bye, little beach shack. Good-bye!"

"What will you do with it?" Mr. Van Legge asked.

Cap'n Jack's eyes flashed excitedly. "Well . . . with all that money, I can buy an *even bigger* beach shack! No—two beach shacks. No—

five or six beach shacks. Wait! I can have beach shacks on every beach in America!"

Mr. Van Legge clapped Cap'n Jack on the back. "I like a man who thinks big."

He turned to Mike and me. "There must be something the Van Legge family can do for you, too."

"Well, can we ride on your ghost schooner?" Mike asked.

"Maybe we shouldn't." I tried to tug Mike back.

"But it would be so awesome!" he said. "Just a short ride?"

"That would be a delight for us all," Mr. Van Legge said. "But I really must tell you that—"

"YAAAY!" Mike cheered. "Thank you! Thank you!"

"But there is something you really need to know. You see—"

"Wow! A ride on a real ghost ship!" Mike cried. "When I get home, no one will believe it. Let's go!"

Annabel and William took our hands. And before I realized what was happening, Mike and I floated off the ground. We sailed into the air and out over the sea.

What a thrill! Gliding over the water like a seabird!

We waved to Cap'n Jack down on the island. He was staring up at us in surprise, scratching his head.

I wanted to keep flying like that forever. But a short while later, we landed on the deck. The ship rocked gently beneath our feet. Mr. Van Legge took the wheel. The rest of us stood along the rail, gazing through the billowing green mist as the schooner set sail.

Up, up, over the lapping waves. As Mr. Van Legge guided the big wheel, the ghost ship rose out of the water and floated into the sky.

Up through the clouds until we could see a million twinkling white stars over the black evening sky.

"This is totally awesome!" Mike exclaimed.

"Yes, it's beautiful," I agreed. "The stars look like sparkling diamonds."

My heart pounding, I held on to the rail and stared all around. Here I am, I thought, sailing in the sky in a ghost schooner from another century!

I didn't want it to end. But I knew it was late. And I knew Mom and Dad must be frantic by now.

I turned away from the rail and stepped up to Mr. Van Legge at the wheel. "Thank you so much," I said. "Mike and I will never forget this ride."

"The pleasure is mine," he replied.

"I'm afraid my parents might be a little worried," I said. "Can you turn around and take us home now?"

He squinted at me. "Home? Well . . . I am afraid I have a little bad news."

I stared back at him. "Bad news?"

He nodded. "I tried to tell you back on the

lighthouse island. You see, I can't turn around. This is a sailing ship. I have to follow the wind."

"But we have to get home!" I cried. "We have to go back."

He shrugged. "I wish we could, Ashley. I most sincerely do. But how do you turn a sailing ship against a wind as strong as this? We have to sail on—forever!"

I stared at him in horror.

He burst out laughing. "I'm sorry. I'm a terrible tease." His eyes twinkled. "I'm an old ghost, and ghosts love to scare people. I can't help it. It's just something I have to do."

I gaped at him. "You mean—?"

"Here—you are home," he said. He pointed down below.

I could see the beach, the dunes, the road behind them, and our summer cottage nes-tled in a clump of pine trees.

"Farewell, and thank you," Mr. Van Legge said, wrapping us in a hug.

"Thank you! Thank you!" all four Van Legges cried. They held Mike and me in a long, ghostly hug. The hug grew tighter, tighter, and suddenly, I saw bright swirls of colors, greens and blues and grays.

Blinking the colors away, I sat up. And found myself on the beach, on my blanket, book in my hand. Had I fallen asleep and dreamed the whole thing?

I gazed out at the lighthouse—and saw the beacon beaming its bright white light out to sea. No. Not a dream. It had all happened.

"Mike—!" I called. "Let's go. We've got to get home—fast!"

"Okay, okay." He came running after me. "But I want to come back to the beach tonight, okay?"

I squinted at him. "Back to the beach? Why?"

"Maybe Cap'n Jack has some more ghost stories."

Recent Books by R.L. Stine

BEWARE! R.L. Stine Picks His Favorite Scary Stories

THE HAUNTING HOUR

NIGHTMARE HOUR

DANGEROUS GIRLS (Coming soon!)

Robert Lawrence Stine is one of the best-selling children's authors in history. He began his writing career at the age of nine, writing short stories, joke books, and comic books for his friends—and has been at it ever since!

After graduating from Ohio State University R.L. moved to New York to become a writer. He wrote joke books and humor books and created *Bananas*, a zany humor magazine, before he turned to the scary. He wrote Fear Street, and then Goosebumps, the phenomenal series that made him an international celebrity and the number-one best-selling children's author of all time (*Guinness Book of World Records*).

He recently published two original collections of scary stories—the *New York Times* best-seller *Nightmare Hour* and *The Haunting Hour*—and a collection of his favorite scary stories of all time—*BEWARE!*

His book series The Nightmare Room was adapted into a popular TV series.

Stine's most recent project, *R.L. Stine's Haunted Lighthouse,* is a 4-D movie which premiered at Busch Gardens and SeaWorld in 2003. R.L. has expanded the story of the film into an original novel for kids, *R.L. Stine's Haunted Lighthouse.*

R.L. lives in Manhattan with his wife, Jane, and their son, Matthew.